Jeanie & Genie

NOT-SO-HAPPY CAMPER

BY **TRISH GRANTED**

ILLUSTRATED BY **MANUELA LÓPEZ**

LITTLE SIMON

New York London Toronto Sydney New Delhi

This book is a work of fiction. Any references to historical events, real people, or real places are used fictitiously. Other names, characters, places, and events are products of the author's imagination, and any resemblance to actual events or places or persons, living or dead, is entirely coincidental.

LITTLE SIMON

An imprint of Simon & Schuster Children's Publishing Division · 1230 Avenue of the Americas, New York, New York 10020 · First Little Simon paperback edition June 2021 Copyright © 2021 by Simon & Schuster, Inc. All rights reserved, including the right of reproduction in whole or in part in any form. LITTLE SIMON is a registered trademark of Simon & Schuster, Inc., and associated colophon is a trademark of Simon & Schuster, Inc. For information about special discounts for bulk purchases, please contact Simon & Schuster Special Sales at 1-866-506-1949 or business@simonandschuster.com. The Simon & Schuster Speakers Bureau can bring authors to your live event. For more information or to book an event contact the Simon & Schuster Speakers Bureau at 1-866-248-3049 or visit our website at www.simonspeakers.com. Designed by Brittany Fetcho Manufactured in the United States of America 0421 MTN 10 9 8 7 6 5 4 3 2 1 Library of Congress Cataloging-in-Publication Data Names: Granted, Trish, author. | López, Manuela, 1985- illustrator. Title: Not-so-happy camper / by Trish Granted ; illustrated by Manuela López. Description: First Little Simon paperback edition. | New York : Little Simon, [2021] | Series: Jeanie & genie ; #4 | Audience: Ages 5-9. | Audience: Grades K-1. | Summary: Jeanie and Willow pinkie-promise not to make or grant any wishes when they go camping together, but when Willow meets Jeanie's camping friends, the genie-in-training wishes the bossy twins would just go away. Identifiers: LCCN 2021007784 (print) | LCCN 2021007785 (eBook) | ISBN 9781534486966 (paperback) | ISBN 9781534486973 (hardcover) | ISBN 9781534486980 (eBook) Subjects: CYAC: Best friends—Fiction. | Friendship—Fiction. | Camping—Fiction. | Wishes—Fiction. | Genies—Fiction. Classification: LCC PZ7.1.G728 No 2021 (print) | LCC PZ7.1.G728 (eBook) | DDC [Fic]—dc23 LC record available at https://lccn.loc.gov/2021007784 LC eBook record available at https://lccn.loc.gov/2021007785

TABLE OF CONTENTS

Chapter 1

PINKIE PROMISE

"Tent? Check. Field notebook? Check. Mosquito net? Check." Jeanie Bell ticked off the items on her packing list.

Jeanie and her family were going camping that weekend, and she couldn't wait. There was nothing like the great outdoors. Even better, Jeanie's best friend, Willow Davis, was coming with them!

1

Actually, Willow was at Jeanie's house at that moment.

Although they weren't leaving for a few more days, Jeanie had already started organizing her camping supplies. Tidy stacks of items covered the living room carpet, organized by category and season.

She'd lined up all her nature books alphabetically and rolled her sleeping bag neatly. And she was just laying out her binoculars and magnifying glass when a small hand reached out from a "tent" made of blankets and couch cushions.

"Touch that magnifying glass and you'll regret it, Jake!" Jeanie warned.

"You're no fun, Meanie Jeanie," Jake called from inside the tent.

Jeanie shook her head. There was one thing she'd like to leave at home this weekend: her little brother!

Jeanie turned to Willow. "You're going to love camping," she said. "We hike and sing songs and go canoeing at Big Bear Lake. And at night we tell stories around the campfire and look at the constellations."

"Gazing at the stars *is* pretty magical," Willow said with a wink.

As long as no one wishes on them! Jeanie thought.

The truth was . . . her friend Willow didn't just know a *few* things about stars. She knew a *lot* of things about stars *and* other magical subjects.

Because . . . Willow was a genie! Or at least a genie-in-training. Willow knew which days of the month were the luckiest and she studied magic color charts. But she was still learning to control her wish-granting skills, and sometimes her magic didn't quite work out the way she intended.

So Jeanie planned to be extra careful this weekend. She didn't want any wayward wishes ruining their camping trip.

"You'll also get to meet my best camping friends, the Berriman twins," Jeanie added.

9

"I hope we see a painted lady butterfly," Willow said as she flipped through Jeanie's books. She held up one with a giant spruce tree on the cover. "What are you bringing this book for?"

"To help me identify different trees," explained Jeanie. "I always collect bark rubbings. It's one of my favorite parts of camping."

"*My* favorite part is making s'mores," Jake called from inside his tent.

"What are s'mores?" asked Willow.

Jake's head popped out. "You've never had a s'more? It's the most awesome dessert ever!"

Jeanie had to agree. "Roasted marshmallows and chocolate in a graham cracker sandwich. Yum!"

"*Oh*," Willow said. Then she paused. "How do you roast marshmallows?"

Jake grinned. "You jab them onto the end of a stick and hold them over the campfire."

Jeanie rolled her eyes. "You're too little for that, Jake. Mom and Dad do the roasting," she reminded her brother.

He shrugged. "Yeah, but I do the eating!"

Willow still looked a little confused. "Why do they call them s'mores?"

"Because, once you taste one, you'll want s'more!" Jake shouted. He cackled, grabbed Jeanie's magnifying glass, and bolted up the stairs to his room.

"Want me to get Jake back for you?" Willow asked. "It's only a wish away. . . ."

"YES!" Jeanie blurted out. Then she took a deep breath. "I mean, no. I have this weekend all planned out, and we don't want to get off track. In fact, let's make a pact: While we're camping, I won't make any wishes and you won't grant any. Pinkie promise?"

Willow smiled. "Pinkie promise!"

FLASHLIGHTS OR FLOWER CROWNS?

On Saturday morning Willow woke up early. Very early.

"Hello there, Mr. Sun!" she said as she bounced out of bed. "You get right to work, don't you!"

Willow usually liked to sleep in. But this weekend was different. She was going camping for the first time.

All week long Willow had daydreamed about the trip, her

imagination running wild. She pictured marshmallow waterfalls, forest fairies chasing rainbow-colored frogs, and a choir of squirrels and bunnies singing to the stars. Basically, the most magical trip ever!

But Willow knew she couldn't make any of that magic happen.

Jeanie said no wishes, she reminded herself as her mom drove her over to the Bells' house. *And pinkie promises are unbreakable!*

Willow was sure they'd still have plenty of fun.

She grabbed her tie-dye duffel bag and ran up the driveway, waving to Mr. and Mrs. Bell, who were busily packing the car.

"You're here!" Jeanie cried, opening the door before Willow even got up the steps. "What's in *there*?" Jeanie had clearly spotted Willow's overstuffed bag.

Willow's eyes lit up. "Oh, you know, just the essentials: my stuffed unicorn, Opal; glitter glue; ribbons to add to our flower crowns; two kaleidoscopes; friendship bracelet supplies; scented candles; and firefly jars," she explained.

Jeanie giggled. "Um, I think you may have packed for the wrong trip!"

"What do you mean?" asked Willow.

"Well, I'm not sure we're going to be using glitter glue or scented candles," Jeanie said, clearly trying to put it gently. "We need to make sure there's room in your bag for some practical necessities. It's best to be prepared. Come on," she said, waving Willow inside.

In the living room Jeanie put Willow's butterfly net, strawberry-covered sun hat, and flashlight in a neat pile. Then she added sunscreen, bug spray, a compass, and an extra sleeping bag. Everything else went in another pile.

Willow didn't understand how anyone could think glitter glue was non-essential. But Jeanie was the camping expert.

"Thanks," said Willow. "I can't wait to be 'one with nature.' But I'm a little nervous, too. The woods are full of creepy, crawly creatures, and it's going to be really dark at night, and I've never even slept outside before and—"

"We're going to have a great time," Jeanie reassured her. "You'll see. But just in case . . ." She moved Opal to the essential pile.

Willow laughed. "It's best to be prepared!"

TWIN-TERRUPTION

A few hours and a lot of car-ride games later, the Bells—and Willow—arrived at the campsite.

Then Jeanie, Willow, and Jake unloaded the car while Mr. and Mrs. Bell set up the tents.

"I think that's a red cedar," Jeanie said, pointing to a tall tree a few feet away. "Let's help get these tents up so we can start rubbing some bark!"

29

"I can sketch the leaves for you," offered Willow. "If you want."

"Definitely," said Jeanie. "Then we can go for a hike or take the canoe out on the lake. But first, we have to gather some firewood."

The girls secured the last tent pole, dusted themselves off, and headed toward the woods to begin their hunt.

"We need lots of small sticks, some branches, and a few big logs to make the perfect campfire," said Jeanie. "And they all have to be super dry."

Willow shielded her eyes. "Mr. Sun sure is shining brightly today," she said. "I hope I don't burn. Red is not my color—"

"Jeanie!" a voice interrupted Willow.

"Over here!" a second voice chimed in.

Jeanie spun around and spotted two identical girls with identical blond ponytails. They were wearing matching outfits and cross-body pouches. It was the Berriman twins! Jeanie hadn't seen them since last summer.

"Hi, Becca! Hi, Bonnie!" Jeanie greeted them. "I was just gathering some firewood."

"Oh, we've already done that," said Becca.

Bonnie gave her sister a high five. "Now we're digging for earthworms so we can go fishing later," she said.

"Last year we caught a dozen trout at Pinecone Falls," Becca added.

Willow cleared her throat.

"Oh, I'm sorry," Jeanie said quickly. "This is my friend Willow. She's never been camping before."

"Never been camping?" Becca exclaimed.

"Ever?" Bonnie's jaw was practically hanging open.

Jeanie thought Willow looked a little embarrassed, so she changed the subject. "Have you guys been up to the lake yet?"

"Yup." Becca pulled a small notepad out of her bag. "And according to the almanac, it's twenty-three percent choppier this year."

"With a breeze coming from the northeast," added Bonnie.

Soon Jeanie and the twins settled into a long conversation about wind speed, water temperature, and duck migrations.

"If you want to canoe to the sandy beach on the other side of the lake, it's going to require extra paddling at the stern," Becca noted.

"Did you hear that, Willow?" Jeanie asked, turning to her friend. "Looks like we might need Jake to help—"

But Willow was gone!

Chapter 4

GHOSTED

Willow dragged a twig through the dirt. She drew spirals and swirls and a little puppy, who she realized looked sort of sad.

"I know how you feel, pup," Willow said. She'd found a spot to sit beneath some shady trees. She glanced at Jeanie, who was still chatting with the Berriman twins. "Some days just aren't as magical as others," she said.

Becca and Bonnie Berriman were outdoor experts, just like Jeanie. But they seemed more interested in facts and figures than they did in making a new friend.

The twins had been talking so fast about so many things Willow didn't understand that she'd finally given up trying to follow along. And when her skin had started to feel hot from the sun, she'd slipped away to sit in the shade.

Now, ten minutes later, Jeanie had finally noticed.

"Willow!" she called out as she trotted over. "Why did you leave?"

"You guys were talking a mile a minute," Willow explained. "And I needed to get out of the sun."

"Is everything okay now?" Jeanie glanced back at the twins. "Because I invited Becca and Bonnie to have s'mores with us tonight. But I need to check with my mom to make sure we have enough marshmallows!"

Willow could see how much it meant to Jeanie, so she gave her a reassuring smile. "Sure. Let's go!"

Back at the campsite, while Jeanie checked in with her parents, Willow tried to cheer herself up. *You love making new friends,* she thought. *Just be your smiley, sunny self!*

Then suddenly she spotted two orange monarchs flitting around some pretty purple wildflowers as if they didn't have a care in the world.

"Look, Jeanie!" Willow pointed as her friend came over. "They're dancing! I bet in a minute they'll do the foxtrot!"

"Huh?" Jeanie mumbled. "Oh, the butterflies? That's nice."

"What did your mom say about the s'mores?" Willow asked.

"We have to wait until tomorrow," said Jeanie. "Mom just wants it to be our family tonight."

Willow felt a rush of relief. She didn't want to be greedy, but she was kind of glad to have Jeanie all to herself.

But Willow couldn't help noticing that Jeanie definitely seemed a little disappointed.

Jeanie didn't spout any interesting facts as they collected bark rubbings for her scrapbook. Or make sure they were watching at the exact moment the sun set. Or join the shadow-puppet play Willow performed while Jeanie's parents got dinner set up.

As they ate, Willow tried to cheer Jeanie up with a joke. "How did the hot dog ask the ketchup to marry him? He *mustard* up the courage!"

Jeanie smiled, but she clearly was only *half* paying attention.

Suddenly Jake stood up in front of the fire and held a flashlight under his chin.

"I'm going to tell the scariest story ever!" he announced.

"Oh no," Jeanie muttered. "First the twins couldn't come over, and now this?"

"Did you know," Jake began in a quivery, shivery voice, "that this place is called Big Bear Lake because of the ghost of a giant grizzly . . ."

GHOST? Willow's eyes went wide. She was a genie, but that didn't mean she was okay with *ghosts*!

First her best friend was ignoring her, and now there might be ghosts? This camping trip was not turning out how Willow had expected . . . at *all*.

MISSION METEOR SHOWER

The next morning Jeanie woke up bright and early. She had lots of things on her to-do list, and nothing was going to stop her from checking off every one of them.

First, she needed to talk to the Berriman twins. Her mom had promised they'd have plenty of extra s'mores at lunch today.

Plus, Jeanie had read that there

was going to be a meteor shower that night. Becca and Bonnie had hiked every inch of Big Bear Lake. They'd know the best spot to get a good view of the stars.

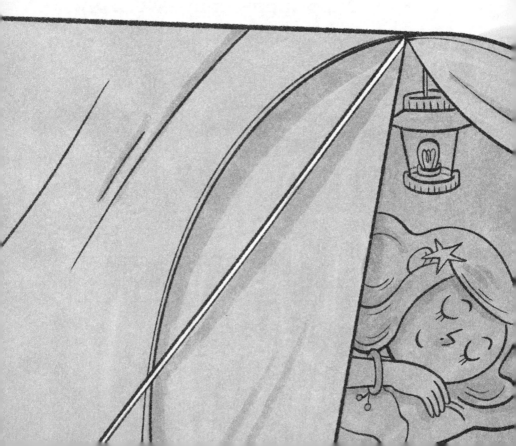

But Jeanie didn't want to wake Willow. She knew her friend liked to dream as long as possible. So she dressed quietly, slipped out of the tent, and hurried over to the Berrimans' campsite.

Becca and Bonnie were more than happy to help.

"There's a big open space near Pinecone Falls," Becca told Jeanie. "We'll be able to see the whole sky from there."

"I brought a telescope from home," Bonnie added.

As the girls chatted, Jeanie thought about how much Willow would enjoy talking about meteor showers and moon phases. Maybe she should have woken Willow up after all? But Jeanie's thoughts were interrupted.

"Here, Jeanie," said Bonnie. "You and Willow can borrow these books about outer space."

"Thanks, guys!" said Jeanie. "I'll see you at lunch."

So far, today was going exactly as Jeanie had planned. She couldn't wait to tell Willow!

But when she got back to the tent, Willow was brushing Opal's mane and looking kind of glum.

"Where were you?" she asked Jeanie.

"With the Berrimans," Jeanie said. "You'll never guess what we're doing today!"

"Looking for butterflies?" Willow said hopefully.

"Better!" cried Jeanie. "There's going to be a meteor shower tonight. Look at all these books Becca and Bonnie lent us. With a little research, we'll know exactly what to look for. Doesn't that sound fun?"

"I guess so," Willow said.

Jeanie frowned. She wished Willow seemed a little more excited. Could she . . . should she . . . wish for that? But she caught herself. There weren't going to be any wishes on this camping trip. They had pinkie-promised.

THE PERFECT S'MORE

Willow and Jeanie spent the rest of the morning talking about the stars.

Well, *Jeanie* spent the morning talking. She rambled on about which constellations Becca thought they'd see, whether Bonnie thought the sky would be dark enough, and how awesome their telescope was.

Willow didn't want to talk about the stars . . . or the twins. And she was still a little hurt that Jeanie had gotten up early and left without her. But she didn't want to make Jeanie feel bad. So while Jeanie pored over the books the twins had given her, Willow daydreamed about the gooey marshmallows and melty chocolate that would be waiting for them at lunch. If s'mores were as good as Jeanie and Jake had promised, she had something seriously sweet to look forward to.

But when lunchtime actually rolled around, Willow realized she'd forgotten one very important thing: The Berrimans were joining them.

It wasn't that Willow didn't like the twins, exactly. They just seemed to be everywhere!

As they began to make s'mores, Becca snapped up the fluffiest marshmallows. And Bonnie grabbed the last piece of milk chocolate, so Willow had to settle for dark.

Then the twins sat on either side of Jeanie, so Willow had to sit all alone.

Willow speared a marshmallow and shoved her stick into the fire.

"You're holding it too close," Becca told Willow. "Keep your stick two inches from the flame to get the best results."

"Counterclockwise rotation is key!" agreed Bonnie.

They're so opinionated, thought Willow.

"You're right!" Jeanie gushed as she pulled an evenly toasted marshmallow from her stick and sandwiched it between two graham crackers. "The perfect s'more!"

Willow stubbornly held her marshmallow in the center of the flames . . . until it oozed off the end and landed on a log with a slimy *plop!* Soon it was a black, sticky mess.

"Looks like yours isn't a s'more," said Becca. "It's a no more!"

Everyone laughed. Everyone except Willow.

"You should have tried it our way," said Bonnie.

Jeanie nodded. Then she asked the twins about their telescope, and soon they were debating ideal magnification settings and optimal stargazing angles.

Willow's cheeks felt hot. Jeanie never usually left her out of things. But ever since she'd been reunited with the Berriman twins, it was like Willow barely existed.

The back of Willow's neck began to prickle as she watched Jeanie talking to Becca and Bonnie. A sudden desire filled her mind, so quick and so strong, Willow couldn't keep it inside:

I wish the twins would just go away!

THE DISAPPEARING ACT

"It says here that meteors rarely land on Earth," Jeanie said.

She'd had her nose buried in one of Becca's books all afternoon.

"They burn up in the atmosphere way before that," Jeanie continued. "And the bright streak of a shooting star isn't the burning rock, it's the hot air whizzing along behind it."

She looked up, expecting to

see Willow's eyes sparkling with curiosity.

Instead all she saw was Willow continuing to lazily weave a daisy chain.

"Earth to Willow," said Jeanie. "Can you believe it? We're finally going to see a shooting star! You always say they're supposed to be extra magical, right?"

"Sure," Willow said. "Magical."

Jeanie gave Willow a concerned look. "Is everything okay?" she asked. "You seem a little . . . down."

81

"I know you're excited about the meteor shower . . . but I was hoping we could look for some butterflies today," Willow admitted. She sounded shy, which was not like her at all!

Jeanie sighed. She really wanted to make sure she was ready for tonight. But she *did* want to go searching for butterflies with Willow too. And Willow had done everything Jeanie wanted to do so far today.

"Okay!" Jeanie said as she closed the book she'd been reading. "I'd love to get a better look at those monarchs you saw yesterday."

She stood and pointed to the stack of books the Berrimans had lent her. "But first, let's go return those. Can you grab our butterfly nets?"

"Does a ladybug have spots?" Willow said with a grin. "Of course I can! And look." She lifted her palm to show Jeanie what lay inside. "I made some itsy-bitsy daisy crowns for the butterflies!"

Jeanie laughed. Willow certainly had imagination. It was one of the things Jeanie loved about her.

The girls gathered everything they needed and set out for the twins' campsite.

But when they got there, the Berrimans were nowhere to be found.

Jeanie scanned the empty campsite. The telescope was gone. The fishing poles were gone. Even the tents were gone. The place was totally deserted.

Becca and Bonnie had just . . . disappeared!

Chapter 8

WILLOW'S BIG MISTAKE

Willow couldn't believe it. No Berrimans meant no more nature quizzes, no more rules to follow, and no more fighting for Jeanie's attention! It was almost too good to be true!

But suddenly Willow's stomach dropped. She'd been so miserable at lunch that she'd wished the twins would go away. And now they had!

89

Whistling wind chimes! It can't be, she thought. *Mom says genie magic doesn't work like that!*

Willow's mom would know—she was the director of the World Genie Association. She'd always taught Willow that genies couldn't grant their own wishes. *Or* make any evil wishes come true.

So why did it seem like that was exactly what had happened?

Willow's heart sank. She didn't know how she was going to tell Jeanie she'd accidentally broken her pinkie promise.

But first she had to find the Berrimans. Saying sorry didn't matter if you weren't trying to make things right.

Jeanie looked around. "Where could they be?" she wondered.

"Maybe they went canoeing?" Willow suggested.

"With all their stuff?" Jeanie shook her head.

"We could go look for them down by the lake instead of going butterfly hunting . . . ," Willow said hesitantly.

"That's okay," said Jeanie. "I'm sure they didn't just *disappear*."

But Willow wasn't so sure of that.

"Let's go hike the Sunflower Loop," said Jeanie, totally unaware of the fact that Willow was panicking inside. "It's the best trail around for butterfly spotting," she added.

The girls spent the next two hours watching swallowtails sip from honeysuckle blossoms, and painted ladies chase each other around a small creek.

Willow tried to have a good time. The butterflies were as pretty as a summer rainbow. And Jeanie knew tons of interesting facts about where they flew and how they got their names.

But Willow couldn't help looking for identical blond ponytails around every bend in the trail. She hoped the Berriman twins were just digging for more earthworms or hiking up Pinecone Falls.

Willow had thought her wish-granting skills were getting stronger. But if she'd accidentally broken the WGA's guidelines, she'd never become a master genie. Why did magic have to be so unpredictable?

By the time they'd reached the end of the trail, Willow had come to a decision. She'd have to be honest about her wish. It was the right thing to do.

She just hoped Jeanie could forgive her.

Chapter 9

THE LETTER

"Monarchs smell using their antennae," Jeanie told Willow as they plopped down into two folding chairs at their campsite. "But they taste with little hairs on their legs and feet. Can you believe it?"

"Wow!" said Willow. She sat on her hands to stop herself from fidgeting. "Listen, I really need to tell you something—"

"Hi, girls!" Jeanie's mom called out. "The Berriman twins stopped by while you were gone. Their mother had something urgent come up for work, so the whole family had to leave. I'm sorry—I know you were having fun with them. But they left you this note."

Jeanie took the letter from her mother, and read it out loud:

Dear Jeanie and Willow,

We're sorry we had to leave early this year. But we had lots of fun at lunch. And we're SO glad we got to meet you, Willow!

We left our telescope so you can use it to look at the stars tonight. We'll get it back from you next time we see you both. ☺

XOXO,
Becca and Bonnie

"They're happy they got to meet me?" Willow asked. "To be honest, I didn't think they liked me very much."

Jeanie looked at her friend. She felt awful that Willow thought that! But then she remembered something. "You know, I thought that the first time I met them too," Jeanie admitted. "I think sometimes they try to impress people because they think then people will like them."

Willow nodded. "That makes sense," she said. "And they do know a lot about nature!"

"Yeah, they do," said Jeanie. "But they love learning new things too! I taught them about tree identification last trip. Maybe next time you can teach them everything you know about stars!"

Willow's eyes got big. "I could do star charts for them," she offered.

Jeanie nodded and said, "I bet they'd like to know every little detail."

"I am sorry they left," said Willow. "I hope that doesn't ruin the rest of our camping trip. I know how excited you were to hang out with them. . . ."

Jeanie smiled. "Yeah, but not as excited as I was to share this whole camping experience with you."

Willow brightened. It was the happiest Jeanie had seen her yet.

"You know, there's still one more thing we haven't done," Jeanie added, a mischievous twinkle in her eye. "And I think you're going to think it's pretty *cool*," she said.

Chapter 10

POLAR BEAR PLUNGE

"This is not what I imagined when you said we were going to do something cool," Willow said.

She couldn't believe she was about to jump into a freezing cold lake. But Jeanie had told her that no camping trip was complete without doing a "polar bear plunge." So here Willow was, standing on the dock, about to jump.

"Ready?" Jeanie asked.

Willow checked to make sure the fuzzy towels they'd brought were still waiting on shore. Then she nodded. "As ready as I'll ever be."

"Let's do it together, okay?" Jeanie said, grabbing her hand. "One, two, three, JUMP!"

The girls leaped off the dock with a gleeful shriek.

As soon as Willow hit the ice-cold water, she understood why they called this the polar bear plunge. Her fingers and toes felt like icicles!

The shock of the cold made a little burst of laughter bubble up inside her. And her giggles were contagious. Soon she and Jeanie were both laughing so hard they were practically crying.

Finally, they calmed down long enough to swim to shore and dry off. As Willow wrapped a fuzzy towel around herself and followed Jeanie back toward their campsite, she felt a pang of sadness that the camping trip was coming to an end.

Last night they'd sat in the big open space near Pinecone Falls and watched the meteor shower. Everything from the hooting owls and tickling breeze to the sparkly shooting stars streaking across the night sky had made Willow feel lucky to be there.

They'd stayed up late telling stories, singing songs, and making up dances. Well, Jeanie had watched as Willow made up dances.

And today they'd spent the morning drawing pictures of butterflies. Jeanie had labeled hers with scientific names, while Willow had sketched a magical butterfly garden scene.

As they packed up, Willow thought about how the trip hadn't started out so great, but it had turned out to be *totally* amazing. And she hadn't even granted a single wish! Nature was pretty magical all on its own!

Suddenly Willow had a great idea.

"Jeanie, do you think your parents have packed up the food yet?" she asked as the girls rolled up their sleeping bags.

"I'm not sure," said Jeanie. "But I can check. Why?"

Willow grinned. "After that freezing dip in the lake, we deserve a treat. How about s'more s'mores?"

It was a perfectly sweet ending to a camping trip they'd never forget.

LOOK FOR MORE

Jeanie & Genie

BOOKS AT YOUR FAVORITE STORE!